Rotherham Schools Loan Service
Maltby Library,
High Street, Maltby, Rotherham S66 8LD.

This book must be returned by the date specified at the time of issue as
the DUE DATE FOR RETURN
The loan may be extended (personally, by post, telephone or online) for
a further period, if the book is not required by another reader, by quoting
the barcode / author / title.

Enquiries: 01709 813034

www.rotherham.gov.uk/sls

Welcome to the Disney Learning Programme!

Sharing a book with your child is the perfect opportunity to cuddle and enjoy the reading experience together. Research has shown that reading aloud to and with your child is one of the most important ways to prepare them for success as a reader. When you share books with each other, you help strengthen your child's reading and vocabulary skills as well as stimulate their curiosity, imagination and enthusiasm for reading.

In this book, Arlo the dinosaur is scared of everything. One day, a series of events leads him to leave the safety of home and confront his fears. When his new companion Spot is in danger, Arlo has to find the courage to save his friend. You can help your child enjoy the story even more by talking to them about times that they have been scared and how they managed to overcome their fear. You can tell your child about how you have overcome your fears, too! Children find it easier to understand what they read when they can connect it with their own personal experiences.

Children learn in different ways and at different speeds, but they all require a supportive environment to nurture a lifelong love of books, reading and learning. The Adventures in Reading books are carefully levelled to present new challenges to developing readers. They are filled with familiar and fun characters from the wonderful world of Disney to make the learning experience comfortable, positive and enjoyable.

Enjoy your reading adventure together!

Scholastic Children's Books
Euston House,
24 Eversholt Street,
London NW1 1DB, UK

A division of Scholastic Ltd
London • New York • Toronto • Sydney • Auckland
Mexico City • New Delhi • Hong Kong

This book was first published in the United States in 2015
by Random House Children's Books, a division of Penguin Random House LLC.
This edition published in the UK by Scholastic Ltd, 2016.

ISBN 978 14071 6609 4

Printed in Malaysia

2 4 6 8 10 9 7 5 3 1

Papers used by Scholastic Children's Books are made from woods grown in sustainable forests.

www.scholastic.co.uk

The Journey Home

ADVENTURES IN READING

By Bill Scollon

Illustrated by

the Disney Storybook Art Team

Arlo is a dinosaur.
He lives with his family on a farm.

Arlo is scared of many things. He is afraid to leave the farm.

One day Arlo sees a wild boy.
The wild boy scares Arlo and Arlo
runs away.

Arlo and the boy fall into the river.
The water sweeps them away.

Arlo is far from home.
The boy is gone.

Arlo is lost and scared.
Arlo could follow the river to get home.

The boy finds Arlo
and brings him food.
They go into the
woods.

Arlo calls the boy Spot. They have
fun and become friends.

Arlo and Spot get lost.
They get attacked!

A pack of T. rexes saves them.

Arlo and Spot are happy.
They will be home soon.

A human calls to Spot but Spot
stays with Arlo.

Arlo and Spot are attacked again!
Spot is trapped in a log.

This time, Arlo is brave.
He fights to help Spot.

A flash flood is coming!
It almost carries Spot away.

Arlo jumps into the water.
He will save his friend!

Arlo and Spot go over a waterfall.
They swim safely to shore.

Arlo and Spot meet a human family.
The friends say a sad goodbye.

Arlo is a brave dinosaur.
He gets home on his own!

ACTIVITIES TO SHARE WITH YOUR CHILD

Now that you've shared the book with your child, encourage them to try these fun activities with you to strengthen their understanding of the story and its themes.

HELPING

During Arlo's adventure, he meets all sorts of creatures. Point to the creatures that help him. Now point to the creature that is not so helpful.

FEELINGS

Arlo's adventure is full of danger as well as fun.
Look at the pictures. How do you think Arlo is feeling?

Use the words below to help you.

scared   joyful   angry   sad

DANGERS

Look at the pictures.
Which situation do you think is the scariest?

FRIENDSHIP
Point to the picture that matches each sentence.

Arlo meets Spot.

Arlo loses Spot.

Arlo and Spot are friends.

Arlo and Spot say goodbye.

The Journey Home

What happens in the end?

?

How does Arlo save Spot?

Goodbye!